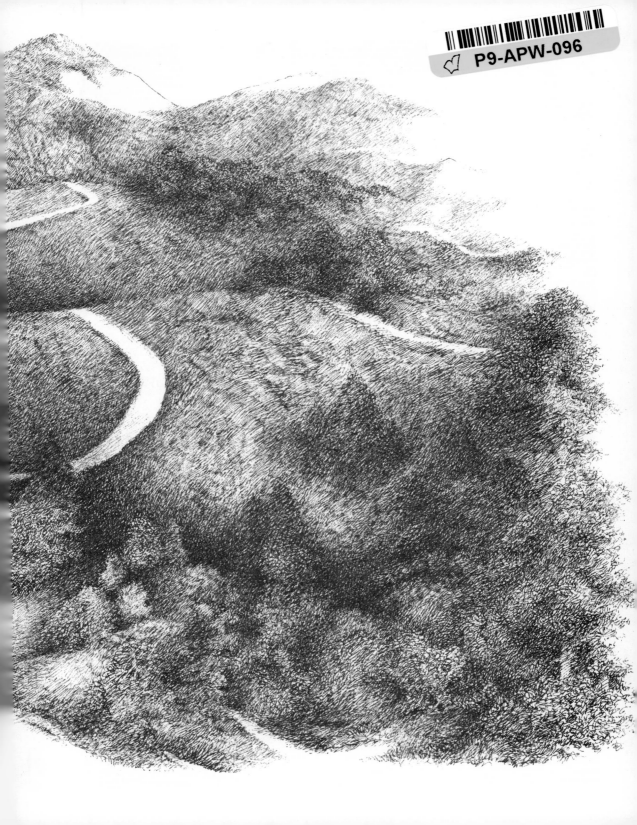

GRANDFATHER'S CAKE

Weekly Reader Books presents

GRANDFATHER'S CAKE

DAVID McPHAIL

Charles Scribner's Sons   New York

Copyright © 1979 David McPhail

Library of Congress Cataloging in Publication Data
McPhail, David M
Grandfather's cake.
SUMMARY: Two brothers and their pony set out to
take a piece of cake to Grandfather and meet several
hungry strangers eager to relieve them of it along the way.
(1. Cake — Fiction) I. Title.
PZ7.M2427Gr   (E)   79-15810
ISBN 0-684-16113-3

Printed in the United States of America

for my uncle, John

PETER AND ANDREW were playing in the
front yard when they heard their
Grandmother calling to them.
      "Peter! Andrew!"

The two brothers went around to the back door to see what Grandma wanted.

"I just baked a chocolate cake," said Grandma, "and I need someone to take a piece to Grandpa."

Now, the boys' Grandfather was way up in the hills tending his flock of sheep. It was a long walk, but the thoughts of having a warm, fresh piece of chocolate cake to keep them company appealed to the boys.

"I'll go!" said Peter.

"No!" shouted Andrew. "Let me take it!"

"You can both go," said Grandma. "You can keep each other company." And she held out a basket covered with a white cloth.

Andrew and Peter grabbed for the basket. *"I'll* carry it!" said Peter.

"No!" said Andrew. "I'll carry it."

"Neither of you will carry it!" said Grandma. "Peaches will! Now go and fetch her!"

Peaches was the family pony. She was kind of mean, and she wasn't the least bit happy about making the trip to see Grandpa.

Peter pulled, and Andrew shoved, and with a great deal of pulling and shoving they managed to get Peaches out of the barn and over to the back door.

"Now, Peaches," said Grandmother as she rubbed the pony's ears and fed her a carrot. "You behave yourself and maybe Grandfather will give you a bite of the apple I've packed in here." Grandmother finished tying the basket onto Peaches's back, then gave her a nudge to start her on her way.

With Peter in the lead, the little expedition moved down the road toward the river.

Across the river, Peter turned left along the forest path. Peter began to whistle, and Andrew hummed, and Peaches seemed to be keeping time to their song with the clop-clippety-clop of her hooves.

All of a sudden a brown fox sprang out of the bushes right in front of Peter!

"Hello, lads," said the fox to the startled boys. "Mind if I walk along with you? These woods are full of robbers and thieves. You just never know when you're going to be set upon."

Peter swallowed and breathed his first breath since the fox had arrived. "Suit yourself," he said, though he wished that the fox would disappear as suddenly as he had appeared.

The fox walked along beside Peaches, staring intently at the basket strapped to her back.

"Whatcha got in the basket, anyway?" he asked finally.

"A piece of chocolate cake for our Grandfather," replied Andrew.

The fox licked his lips and began to drool. "If there's anything I like more than roast chicken," he said, "it's a luscious piece of chocolate cake. Why don't I just take it off your hands." And he lifted the cloth and reached into the basket.

"Why don't you just take *yo'* hands off it!" said a deep voice that seemed to come from a stout beech tree standing just off the path.

The fox jumped back, terrified. "Who said that?" he squealed, not really wanting to know.

"*I* said dat!" roared a big black bear as he stepped out from behind the tree.

With one flick of his paw the huge bear snatched up the frightened fox and dangled him over the brook that tumbled along below the path.

"So long, Foxy," the bear chuckled, and he dropped the fox into the icy stream.

"Waaooooowwwww!!!" yelped the fox as he thrashed and sputtered. He bobbed along like a cork in the fast-moving water and soon disappeared around a sharp bend.

"Now, then," said the bear, slapping his paws together with satisfaction. "No need to trouble yo'selfs any longer wif riff-raff like dat feller. You got *me* to protect you!"

Peter and Andrew smiled and nodded, and once more got Peaches moving toward the hills, and Grandpa.

The bear led the way until they reached the edge of the forest and came to a narrow gap between two piles of boulders.

"Well, here you are," said the bear, "safely delivered out of this evil forest."

"Thank you," said Peter. "We're most grateful."

"Fine," the bear said and laughed. "Then why don't I just take that piece of cake I heered ole Foxy talking about as my payment for a job well done."

The bear was about to reach into the basket when he heard a tremendous BOOM!!

The noise so startled Peter that he fell over backward, and when he looked up, there was a tall masked man standing in the middle of the path a few feet in front of him. In each hand the man held a pistol, and one of the pistols was smoking.

"Touch one crumb of that cake," said the man, "and you're a bearskin rug. Now git!" And he pointed the other pistol right at the bear.

That old bear didn't need to be told twice. Like a frightened puppy, he bounded off down the path and vanished into the forest.

"It's a good thing I came along when I did," said the masked man. "Bears can be dangerous. Maybe I should just tag along with you, in case he decides to come back for that cake. What kind is it, anyway?"

"Chocolate," answered Andrew. "It's for our Grandfather."

When Andrew said "Grandfather," Peaches perked up her ears. Grandpa was the one who would give her a bite of the apple in that basket she was carrying. The basket was very important to Peaches, and she was determined not to let it out of her sight.

Meanwhile, the group had passed through the narrow gap and started up the steep slope of the lower hill. The climb was difficult, and it made Peaches feel all the nastier. By the time they reached the top of the hill, they were all puffing.

"We're almost there," said Peter. "Once we cross the log bridge over the ravine, we should find Grandpa just beyond the next hill."

At the log bridge the tall masked man pulled out his pistols and blocked the way.

"I'm going to lighten your load a little," he said. "I'm going to relieve you of that basket." He shoved one pistol back into his belt and proceeded to untie the basket with his free hand.

The man had nearly loosened the knot when Peaches whirled around and let fly with her back feet. One hoof hit the gun and knocked it into the ravine. The other hoof landed with a wicked thud right in the man's belly.

"OOOHUMMPFF!!" the man groaned and fell to the ground. When he rolled over and looked up, there was Peaches—feet firmly planted, ready to let him have it again.

The man tucked his head onto his chest and rolled like a lopsided ball all the way back down the hill. Then he got up and wobbled through the gap toward the forest.

"The bear will probably be happy to see him again," said Peter.

"Especially since he left his guns here," observed Andrew as he picked up the other pistol and threw it into the ravine.

"I've been thinking," said Peter, "about that cake, I mean. We've gone through a lot of trouble to bring a piece of cake all the way up here. Suppose, just suppose, that somebody eats that cake before it gets to Grandpa..."

"We could tell him that a fox ate it," said Andrew. "Or a bear."

"Or even a robber," said Peter.

The two brothers sat on the log bridge for a long time just thinking about that delicious chocolate cake.

"But Grandpa will be very disappointed," said Peter after giving the matter a lot of thought.

"So will Grandma," added Andrew. "She made the cake especially for him."

Peter walked over to Peaches and tightened the rope that held the basket. Then he led her across the ravine and up the hill. Andrew got up and followed along.

The boys' Grandfather was already headed for home with his little flock when he spied Peter, Peaches, and Andrew walking up the hill toward him. He waved and called to them. When Peaches heard Grandpa's voice, she broke into a trot, and Peter and Andrew had to run to keep up.

"I'm happy to see you," said Grandpa as he hugged the boys, "but what brings you all the way up here?"

"Grandma baked a cake," answered Peter. "And she asked us to bring a piece to you."

Andrew untied the basket and placed it at his Grandfather's feet. Grandpa lifted the cloth and peered into the basket. His eyes widened and he smiled.

"Why, there are THREE pieces of cake here," he said, "and a shiny red apple!!"

The illustrations for *Grandfather's Cake*
were drawn in pen and ink
and reproduced in a 200 line screen dropout
halftone.
The text type is Bauer Text 1761, photocomposition,
with display in Hadriano Stonecut.

Designed by Diana Hrisinko